PEANUTS®
A Charlie Brown
THANKSGIVING

By Charles M. Schulz
Based on the animated special, the text was adapted by Daphne Pendergrass
Illustrated by Scott Jeralds

Simon Spotlight
New York   London   Toronto   Sydney   New Delhi

SIMON SPOTLIGHT
An imprint of Simon & Schuster Children's Publishing Division
1230 Avenue of the Americas, New York, New York 10020
This Simon Spotlight edition September 2016
SIMON SPOTLIGHT and colophon are registered trademarks of Simon & Schuster, Inc. For information about special discounts for bulk purchases, please contact Simon & Schuster Special Sales at 1-866-506-1949 or business@simonandschuster.com. Manufactured in China 0616 LEO
10 9 8 7 6 5 4 3 2 1   ISBN 978-1-4814-6805-3   ISBN 978-1-4814-6806-0 (eBook)

THIS BOOK BELONGS TO

Brett

It's Thanksgiving, and Charlie Brown's friend Lucy can't wait to celebrate.

"Charlie Brown! I'll hold this football, and you kick it!" Lucy says.

"You can't fool me," says Charlie Brown. "I'll come running up, and you'll pull the football away like you always do."

"But one of the best traditions is the Thanksgiving football game," says Lucy, "and the most important part is the kickoff!"

Charlie Brown thinks Lucy will let him kick the football if it's a holiday tradition. He runs toward the football . . . but she pulls it away—again.

Later, Charlie Brown is talking with his sister, Sally, and his friend Linus.

"Why should I give thanks on Thanksgiving?" Sally asks. "I haven't even finished eating my Halloween candy yet. Besides, all Thanksgiving does is make more work for us in school!"

Linus disagrees. "Thanksgiving is a very important holiday," he explains. "Ours was the first country in the world to make a national holiday to give thanks."

Sally sighs and stares lovingly at Linus. "Isn't he the cutest thing?"
Linus just rolls his eyes. "What are you going to do on Thanksgiving, Charlie Brown?"

"Sally and I are going over to our grandmother's house for dinner," Charlie Brown says.

As soon as they get back home, Charlie Brown gets a call from Peppermint Patty.

"My dad said I could join you for Thanksgiving," she says. "I don't mind inviting myself over, since I know you kind of like me, Chuck."

Charlie Brown tries to explain that he is going to his grandmother's house for dinner, but Peppermint Patty keeps talking over him!

"By the way, I told Marcie and Franklin about the big turkey dinner you're having, so you can count on three for dinner."

"Peppermint Patty has invited herself, Marcie, and Franklin over for Thanksgiving dinner, and I'm not even going to be home!" Charlie Brown groans to Linus.

Linus has an idea. "You can have two dinners: Cook the first one for your friends, and then go to your grandmother's house with your family for the second one."

But there's one flaw to Linus's plan: Charlie Brown doesn't know how to cook.
"All I can make is cold cereal and toast!" Charlie Brown admits.
Linus isn't discouraged. "Maybe we could help," he says. "Snoopy, go out to
the garage and get a table for the backyard."
Snoopy salutes Linus and gets to work.

Snoopy and Woodstock find an old Ping-Pong table, and they bring it outside. Then Snoopy sets up chairs around the table—lawn chairs, beach chairs, rocking chairs—enough for everyone. To top it off, they add a pretty tablecloth, set the table, and even fold the napkins for each place setting.

Now that the table is ready, Snoopy, Woodstock,
Charlie Brown, and Linus start to make Thanksgiving dinner. Linus and Charlie
Brown set up toasters and put in slices of bread. Once the bread is toasted,
Snoopy butters all the pieces and stacks them on a serving platter.

While Linus and Charlie Brown get popcorn, jelly beans, and pretzels, Snoopy and Woodstock disappear for a minute, and then they return dressed up like Pilgrims!

Charlie Brown isn't impressed. "How can you serve the food in that ridiculous outfit?" he scolds Snoopy. "The guests will be here soon!"

Snoopy sighs and reaches for his chef's hat.

Soon, Peppermint Patty, Marcie, and Franklin arrive and follow Charlie Brown out to the big table in the backyard. It's time for dinner! Snoopy is about to serve the guests when Peppermint Patty cuts in.

"Shouldn't we say grace first?" she asks.

Linus stands up. "In the year 1621, the Pilgrims had their first Thanksgiving feast," he begins. "Elder William Brewster, who was a minister, said a prayer that went something like this: 'We thank God for our homes and food and our safety in a new land. We thank God for the opportunity to create a new world for freedom and justice!'"

"Amen!" Peppermint Patty says.

Snoopy lifts the lid off a big platter and reveals the feast: freshly popped popcorn, colorful jelly beans, salty pretzel sticks, and a stack of hot buttered toast. He loads up each guest's plate and sends it sailing over to them.

Peppermint Patty frowns. "What kind of Thanksgiving dinner is this? Where's the turkey, cranberry sauce, and pumpkin pie, Chuck?" she asks Charlie Brown. "Don't you know anything about Thanksgiving dinners? What blockhead made all this?"

She throws down her popcorn in disgust!

Snoopy pulls his chef's hat down over his face, and Charlie Brown gets up and walks away from the table.

"You were kinda rough on Charlie Brown," Marcie says to Peppermint Patty.

"Rough?" Peppermint Patty shouts. "We were supposed to be served a real Thanksgiving dinner!"

"But did he invite you here?" Marcie asks. "Or did you invite yourself and us, too?"

Peppermint Patty thinks for a minute. She knows Marcie is right. "Marcie, maybe you could go to Chuck and patch things up for me?"

Marcie isn't so sure that's a good idea. "I think maybe you should go to Chuck and tell him yourself," she says.

"I'll just ruin everything. You go and speak for me."

Back in the house, Marcie finds Charlie Brown in the living room, looking upset.

"Peppermint Patty didn't mean all those things she said," Marcie tells him. "Actually, she really likes you."

"I'm just sorry I ruined everyone's Thanksgiving," he moans.

But Marcie knows Charlie Brown is missing the point. "Thanksgiving isn't just about eating," she says. "We should be thankful for being together. That's what Thanksgiving is all about."

Peppermint Patty sneaks up behind the two of them. "Apologies accepted?" she asks, offering to shake hands with Charlie Brown.

Charlie Brown smiles and shakes her hand.

Just then the clock chimes.

"Good grief!" Charlie Brown cries. "It's four o'clock!"

He and Sally are supposed to be at their grandmother's house in half an hour! Charlie Brown picks up the phone and dials his grandmother's number.

Charlie Brown starts to tell his grandmother that they'll be late for dinner because their friends haven't eaten yet, but after a minute, he breaks into a huge grin. Everyone—Charlie Brown, Sally, Franklin, Linus, Peppermint Patty, and Marcie—is invited to Thanksgiving dinner at his grandmother's house!

Peppermint Patty runs to the backyard. "We're all invited to Charlie Brown's grandmother's for Thanksgiving dinner!" she cries. Everyone cheers!

After the gang piles into the car, they settle into their seats and wave good-bye to Snoopy and Woodstock.

"Isn't there an old song about going to a grandmother's house?" Marcie asks.

Peppermint Patty nods, and all the kids start to sing, "Over the river and through the woods, to Grandmother's house we go!"

Back at Snoopy's doghouse, Snoopy and Woodstock put the finishing touches on their own Thanksgiving dinner—with pumpkin pie for dessert! Thanksgiving is always special, especially when you celebrate it with friends!